THIS LEVINSON BOOK
BELONGS TO:

_____

_____

First published in Great Britain in 1996 by
Levinson Children's Books, a division of David & Charles Ltd
Greenland Place, 115–123 Bayham Street, London NW1 0AG

10 9 8 7 6 5 4 3 4 2 1

Text copyright © Levinson Children's Books 1996
Illustrations copyright © Alison Bartlett 1996

The right of Alison Bartlett to be identified
as the illustrator of this work has been asserted by her
in accordance with the Copyright Designs and Patents Act 1988.

ISBN 1 899607 52 8 hardback
ISBN 1 86233 027 1 paperback

A CIP catalogue record for this title is available from the British Library.

Printed and bound in Italy.

Cat
among the
cabbages

ALISON BARTLETT

LEVINSON BOOKS

A big white cat sleeps in the hot sun.

He wakes up, stretches lazily
and gives a **long long** yawn.

The big white cat walks through a big blue gate,

leaving a trail of small

blue pawprints.

The cat steps through tangled leaves and tiny green pea pods,

and walks past
neat straight rows of
huge green cabbages.

The cat crouches low on the ground,
sneaking through a field of little yellow flowers.

He leaps!
And a large yellow butterfly
flutters high into the sky.

The cat struts past small pink piglets

running around a
fat pink pig.

He creeps silently past a young brown puppy dog

chewing a very
old brown boot.

The cat walks past a quiet red hen

and a noisy red rooster.

Cock-a-doodle-doooooooooo¡¡¡¡oooo¡¡¡¡

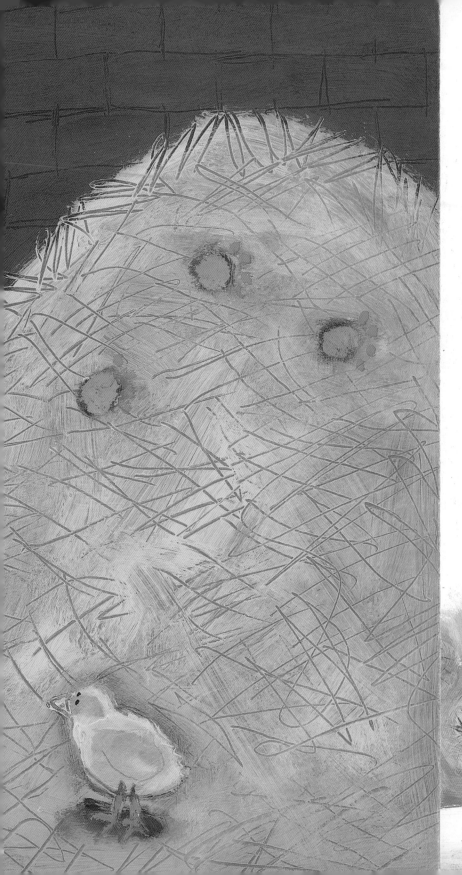

The big white cat stops.
He peers into an **enormous** dark barn.

The big white cat finds a medium-sized black cat,

Follow the cat's walk through the garden, and spot the different colours.

A big white cat sleeps in the hot sun.
He wakes up, stretches lazily and gives a long long yawn.

The white cat walks through a big **blue** gate,
leaving a trail of small **blue** footprints.

The cat steps through tangled leaves and tiny **green** pea pods,
and walks past neat straight rows of huge **green** cabbages.

The cat crouches low on the ground,
sneaking through a field of little **yellow** flowers.
He leaps! And a large **yellow** butterfly flutters high into the sky.

The cat struts past small **pink** piglets,
running around a fat **pink** pig.

He creeps silently past a young **brown** puppy dog
chewing a very old **brown** boot.

The cat walks past a quiet **red** hen,
and a noisy **red** rooster.
Cock-a-doodle-dooooooooo!!!!

The big **white** cat stops. He peers into an enormous dark barn.

The big **white** cat finds a medium-sized **black** cat,
and lots of small **black and white** kittens!